Popcorn-Eating SQUIRRELS Go Nuts with the Dinosaurs

Popcorn-Eating SQUIRRELS Go Nuts with the Dinosaurs

MATT DICKINSON

ILLUSTRATED BY
CALLOWAY BERKELEY O'REILLY

shrine
bell

www.shrinebell.com

PUBLISHER'S NOTE
No squirrels, dinosaurs or babies were harmed in the course of writing this book.

Popcorn-Eating Squirrels Go Nuts with the Dinosaurs
Matt Dickinson

First published in 2020 by Shrine Bell, an imprint of Vertebrate Publishing.

shrine
bell Shrine Bell
Omega Court, 352 Cemetery Road, Sheffield S11 8FT, United Kingdom.
www.shrinebell.com

A CIP catalogue record for this book is available from the British Library.

ISBN 978-1-83981-004-6

10 9 8 7 6 5 4 3 2 1

Design and production by Jane Beagley, Vertebrate Publishing.
Illustration colour work by Cameron Bonser, Vertebrate Publishing.
www.v-publishing.co.uk

Shrine Bell and Vertebrate Publishing are committed to printing on paper from sustainable sources.

Printed and bound in Europe by Latitude Press.

WARNING: Time travel is inherently dangerous. No one should undertake time travel or interact with dinosaurs without the proper training or equipment, and individuals must take personal responsibility for following appropriate safety protocols and employing good judgement. Failure to do so may have many negative implications, including but not limited to being blasted into space, getting eaten alive or changing the entire history of the planet. The author or publisher cannot be held responsible or liable for any damage or injury that may be caused as a result of time travel or dinosaur interaction.

FOR ZOLA

CHAPTER 1

POPTASTIC TIMES!

The good times were rolling (and popping!) for our four squirrel friends:

Ben

Cassie

Alfie

Salty

And the reason was simple:

POPCORN was available in abundance!

Salted

Caramel

Butterscotch

Plain

'This is the life, pals!' Salty exclaimed each evening, as the popcorn-raiding began. 'We're the luckiest squirrels in the world!'

'Alfie happy!' sang Alfie, the smallest of

the four friends. 'Never go hungry ever again!'

Here's the deal. The Popcorn-Eating Squirrels had recently returned from an expedition to Everest and were now secretly living in the roof above the world's leading popcorn-machine manufacturer.

This was the home of the legendary Pop-O-Matic 3000, and Fandango, the eccentric inventor and former magician, was testing improvements on it every single day.

New recipes were being tried. Popcorn was being created and there was hardly anyone there to eat it.

The heavenly snack was there for the taking. Scattered on the floor of the old factory. The bins were overflowing with it. *Popcorn delight!*

'Just make sure we're never seen or heard,' Cassie reminded her friends each evening. 'It only takes one mistake and they'll call in the exterminators.'

Cassie was right to be cautious. Sneaking in the deepest shadows of the night was essential for these popcorn-addicted critters. The team behind the Pop-O-Matic 3000 hated the squirrels with a vengeance and would not take kindly to having sneaky pop-thieves on their premises.

But, so long as they remained
undiscovered, things were:
   Squirrelicious!
   Squirreltastic!
   Squirrelscrumptious!
   And really not bad at all.
   Until, one day, everything changed.
   The popcorn stopped.
   And the hunger began.

CHAPTER 2

DANGEROUS DREAMS

The owner of the factory rushed in,
his eyes shining with a manic glow.

'I've had a dream!' Fandango exclaimed.
'A *glorious* dream!'

The woman behind the desk raised an
eyebrow.

Rosalba.

Rosalba was Fandango's business partner,
heavily made-up – plastered, some might
say – her lips scarlet red, her eyelids dusted
generously with deepest tones of kingfisher
blue. Dangling from her ears were fake
rubies and emeralds which glittered
gaudily in the early morning sunlight.

Around her neck a black velveteen
choker was tightly fastened, adorned with
a single, tarnished, plastic replica pearl.

'A dream?' she replied.

Rosalba coughed. Or was it a sarcastic snort? She was used to the crazed exclamations of her business associate and only very rarely did they come to anything.

'Yes, a dream, my sweet lady.' Fandango plucked Rosalba from her seat and whizzed her round and round at high speed, her faded silk ballgown flapping in the slipstream. 'A stunning and sensational dream!'

'Will it make us rich?' Rosalba asked.

Fandango sat down, dizzied by his efforts. He dabbed at his forehead with a handkerchief.

'Beyond our wildest imaginings!' he exclaimed.

Rosalba smiled dreamily. 'In that case, I approve,' she said. 'So what's the big idea?'

'I'm going to create the Pop-O-Matic 3000 TT,' Fandango declared.

'TT?' Rosalba replied. 'What does TT stand for?'

Fandango's eyes narrowed as he looked about the room. 'We have to be careful of spies,' he said.

He moved closer to whisper in Rosalba's ear.

The squirrels pricked up their ears,
but couldn't hear the murmured words.

'Wow!' Rosalba gasped. 'I never
imagined it was *that*! Do you really think
you can do it?'

'I can! But I need some time to make it
happen,' Fandango added. 'Then we will
conquer the world.'

Fandango retreated to his workshop,
a place so secure that not even the squirrels
could penetrate.

The popcorn testing stopped.

Mysterious boxes arrived. Courier
deliveries from exotic corners of the
world. Gleaming objects emerged, seen
for a tantalising second or two before
vanishing behind closed doors.

Hunger began to bite for the squirrels.

Then began the clanging of hammers,
ringing on steel. The whirring of drills.
The spinning of lathes. The nerve-wrecking
wail of the angle grinder. The sparky
crackle of an oxyacetylene welding

machine. The rasping of a hacksaw.
The whine of an electric screwdriver,
turning endlessly through the night.

The rumble of the squirrels' tummies.

'It's been a week since we ate,' Ben moaned. 'When's he going to start popping again?'

'Maybe we should move on, pals,' Salty said. 'Find a different source of popcorn? My tummy cannae take much more of this.'

'We stay put!' Cassie insisted. 'As soon as Fandango gets that new machine running, the popcorn will start up again, better than ever before.'

The 'TT' part of the project captured the squirrels' imagination. They spent endless hours trying to work out what it meant.

'Terrific Toffee?' Ben guessed.

'Totally Tremendous?' was Cassie's try.

'Tiddlywink Tournament!' cried Alfie.

Then, one magical day, the door of Fandango's workshop burst open.

'I've done it!' he cried.

He pushed a Pop-O-Matic 3000 into the showroom. The minibus-sized machine glittered with highly polished metal,

with a glass canopy sitting snugly on the top.

The squirrels gathered in their hiding place, looking down on the scene, eyes wide, tails twitching.

'It looks very similar to the old one,' Rosalba sniffed.

'Check out the initials!' Fandango said.

He pointed to the gold TT lettering that was emblazoned on the side of the contraption.

'TT!' Cassie whispered. 'If only we knew what it *meant*!'

'Well, you've cracked it in the nick of time,' Rosalba said. 'I've arranged a children's party this afternoon where you can demonstrate it for the very first time to some extremely wealthy clients.'

Fandango rubbed his hands together.

'The wealthier the better,' he said. 'They'll pay any price once they see what this little gem can do!'

The Pop-O-Matic 3000 TT was loaded

on to the back of a truck and the duo set
out for the party.

What they didn't know was that four
stowaways were hiding in the cavity of
the machine.

Our squirrel friends were about to find
out what 'TT' was all about.

CHAPTER 3

COUNTRY LIFE

A vast stately home came into view,
a veritable palace crowned with towers and
turrets, surrounded by glorious gardens.

The squirrels gazed at the mighty
mansion through the glass of the Pop-O-
Matic.

'What a place,' Cassie whispered.

'Fit for a king!' Ben agreed.

Fandango parked the truck in the drive
and the door of the mansion swept open.

A small girl stood there, dressed in a
frilly white dress. Her hair was intricately
set, twisted into ringlets of shining gold.
Her face was also twisted, but not in an
attractive way; it was contorted in an ugly
grimace.

Rosalba stepped from the truck.

'You must be Gertrude,' she gushed. 'It's a real pleasure to—'

'You're late for my party,' the girl snapped. 'It's not acceptable!'

Gertrude's eyes narrowed, her mouth turning down in a sulky fashion and spoiling yet further the impression of the fancy ribbons and curls.

Rosalba and Fandango approached. The young girl looked them up and down.

'I thought party entertainers would be cool and funny and *young*,' she said. 'Not two shrivelled-up old *skeletons*.'

Rosalba picked at her face, rearranging one of her stuck-on eyelashes which had come adrift.

'We're young at heart, sweet girl,' she said sharply. 'And that's what counts.'

A man and a woman emerged from the mansion, dressed in matching tweed suits. They had the healthy skin tone of folk who spend their lives in the great outdoors.

The woman had a baby in her arms, an adorable rosy-cheeked child, gurgling away contentedly.

'I am the Duke of Appleton,' the man said smoothly, 'and this is my wife, the Duchess. I see you've already met our sweet and beloved Gertrude.'

Gertrude gave the baby a poisonous look.

'Can't you stop that baby making that stupid noise?' she snapped. 'It never stops babbling. It's SO annoying!'

'Your little brother loves you,' the Duchess said. 'See how he smiles when he looks at you?'

The baby beamed at his big sister. Gertrude scowled.

'It can't speak properly,' she said. 'It can't even say my name. It's pathetic.'

Gertrude spun around, pulling her parents back into the house.

'Let's get the party started,' she said. 'I'm fed up with all this waiting.'

'Follow on!' the Duke called to Rosalba

and Fandango. 'We'll show you where to set up.'

Five minutes later, the Pop-O-Matic was installed in the ballroom. This was the grandest room in the mansion and it was packed with overexcited children.

Decorated with walls of pink silk, it boasted three spectacular crystal chandeliers and a hundred mirrors which stretched from the floor to the roof. A huge table was groaning beneath the weight of jellies and cream cakes, chocolate fountains and towers of fudge. Thousands of balloons had been inflated and colourful streamers were strung from wall to wall.

'Now this is what I call a *party room*,' Gertrude told Rosalba. 'Can you believe my stupid parents wanted to have a family picnic down by the lake to celebrate my birthday? A picnic! Pah!'

The squirrels were hiding amongst a pyramid of presents in the corner of the ballroom, peeking out at the lively scene.

The baby was placed in a cot next to them. The squirrels could see two twinkling blue eyes staring out from the blankets.

'Alfie wants to tickle the baby,' Alfie said in a whisper. 'Alfie loves babies!'

'Not now,' Cassie muttered. 'Just keep still and stop fidgeting.'

In total, a hundred children had turned up. Dressed in their finest party clothes, they rushed about in crazy zigzags, patting balloons into the air and playing skidsies on the highly polished floor.

The Pop-O-Matic 3000 TT was in the centre of the room, hidden by a golden sheet of the finest cloth.

The Duke suddenly cried out, 'Quiet, everybody!'

The ballroom fell silent.

'I want to introduce our special guests,' he announced. 'Give them a big welcome!'

A ripple of polite applause rang out as Rosalba swept forward, her ballgown swishing around her feet.

'My name is Rosalba,' she announced. 'This is my business associate, Fandango, and THIS is the most magical invention in the world!'

Rosalba pulled back the sheet.

The crowd gasped.

CHAPTER 4
DINOSAUR DESIRES

The young guests clapped their hands as they saw the gleaming shape of the biggest and most fabulous popcorn machine ever designed. Flashing lights on the panels buzzed with gorgeous greens and reds.

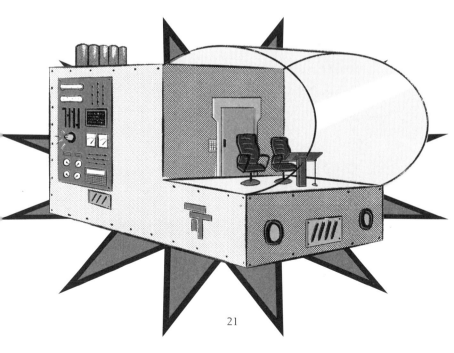

The partygoers emitted a simultaneous 'Oooh!' Gertrude made a little jump in the air, then turned and hugged her parents, tears of joy in her eyes.

'The Pop-O-Matic 3000 TT,' Rosalba announced. 'Popcorn machine of the gods! Now, let me hand over to Fandango to tell you more … '

'Greetings, little ones!' Fandango announced. 'I am Fandango, inventor of this wondrous creation.'

He bowed low to the crowd, low enough that his wig flipped forward to reveal a shiny bald head.

Rosalba flopped it back again with a swift flick of her wrist as he stood back upright.

'Ahem! I've always been aware that the Pop-O-Matic has special powers,' Fandango continued. 'To give you an idea, it once turned a bunch of scabby squirrels into superheroes.'

Over in the pile of gifts, the squirrels'

fur bristled.

Salty scratched at his rump.

'Scabby?' he whispered. 'The cheek of it!'

'Stop scratching!' Cassie hissed. 'Have you got fleas or something?'

'Of course not!' Salty protested.

'Shhh! I'm trying to listen!' Ben told them.

Fandango continued:

'So I started tinkering with the Neutron Generator, added a few Particle Accelerators and Ion Extractors to the Flux Capacitor … and bingo!'

The inventor patted the machine affectionately.

'The Pop-O-Matic 3000 TT. The Pop-O-Matic is now a time machine! The TT part stands for Time Travel.'

The children jumped up and down with excitement.

Over in their secret spot, the squirrels were also thrilled by the news.

'Time machine,' whispered Salty. 'I knew Fandango was a genius, pals, but that's amazing!'

'Awesome!' Cassie agreed.

The Duke bent down on one knee to speak to his precious daughter.

'So now comes the special part for you, Gertrude. Because it's your birthday, I have employed these brave time-travelling adventurers to go back in time and get you any present in the world!'

The children chattered excitedly.

'Any present that has ever existed?' Gertrude raised an eyebrow.

The Duke nodded confidently.

'Anything?' she said.

'Anything!' the Duke replied.

The birthday girl thought for a few moments.

'Get me a dinosaur,' she said.

In their hiding place, the squirrels gasped.

'Alfie loves dinysaurs!' Alfie whispered.

24

'So do I!' Ben muttered.

'Shhhhh!' Cassie scolded. 'Let's listen.'

The confident expression on Rosalba's face faltered for a moment.

'A *what?*' she said.

Fandango shuffled his feet and stared at the floor.

Gertrude's friends squealed with delight.

'A dinosaur!' they cried. 'Brilliant!'

Rosalba and Fandango exchanged a sideways glance. Sweat began to collect on Fandango's brow.

Gertrude crossed to the corner of the ballroom where a series of wooden cabinets was displayed. She slid out a specimen tray and picked out an impressive-looking fossil.

'My father has one of the greatest fossil collections in the world,' she said proudly. 'I've grown up with these dinosaur remains and now I want a real one!'

'Are you sure there's not something else you would like?' Fandango said.

'Y-y-y-yes,' Rosalba gushed rather desperately. 'We were thinking more of a doll from the Victorian era, or a toy made in Roman times, or a special flower perhaps from—'

'I said a *dinosaur*,' the birthday girl snapped. She stamped her foot down hard and folded her arms. 'Now go and find it. And make it a loud roary one so I don't have to listen to the *pathetic* bleatings of my *useless* baby brother!'

CHAPTER 5

DINOSAUR DISAPPOINTMENTS

Fandango wiped perspiration from his face. 'Th-th-th-there are limits,' he stammered. 'And legal implications for insurance and—'

The Duke marched up to the hapless time travellers and rapped his knuckles on the Pop-O-Matic.

'I've paid you two a fortune to keep my sweet little Gertrude happy,' he said. 'So get on with it and don't let me down.'

'Of course,' Rosalba replied with glittering eyes. 'The charming little lady wants a dinosaur; a dinosaur she will have!'

The two ageing entrepreneurs climbed, rather stiffly, into the Pop-O-Matic 3000 TT.

Inside were two seats; in front of them a control panel. Fandango turned a dial. A series of numbers raced across a small screen.

'Sixty-five million years ago,' he muttered. 'The time of the dinosaurs.'

'And don't keep us waiting too long,' Gertrude said curtly.

Rosalba tugged at the glass roof, closing it tight with a metallic click.

'Stand back!' came Fandango's muffled cry from within.

The Pop-O-Matic 3000 TT emitted a clunk. Gears meshed into each other with a steely ring. Something deep inside the works started howling like a turbo-charged tiger.

'Don't get too close,' called the Duke.

The children shuffled back.

The air around the Pop-O-Matic began to crackle with a high-pitched electric fizzing noise.

'Woweeee!' Alfie hissed from the pile of gifts. 'Alfie loves the Pop-O-Matic TT!'

'Shhh!' Cassie placed a paw over Alfie's mouth.

The Pop-O-Matic 3000 TT went a strange shade of pink for a few seconds, then vanished in a puff of lime-green smoke.

Ten minutes passed. Twenty. An hour. The children got bored with waiting and started throwing cocktail sausages at the family's pet cat.

The squirrels were restless as well in their hideaway, especially Salty, who was itching more and more.

Then …

'They're coming back,' cried the Duke.

KPUT!

The Pop-O-Matic rematerialised in the centre of the room. Gloopy mud dripped from it on to the floor. The crowd cheered and clapped.

The partygoers moved towards the Pop-O-Matic.

A hiss of compressed air made the crowd – and the squirrels – gasp. Through a cloud of green steam they saw Rosalba rise, rather shakily, to her feet.

'Whatever happened to you?' the Duke said. 'You look like you've been ten rounds with a prizefighter.'

Rosalba's dress was ripped to shreds, seemingly by something with very big claws. Slimy gloop dripped off her in copious quantities. Her make-up was smudged, her hair a crow's nest.

Rosalba addressed the birthday girl.

'Happy birthday, my dear Gertrude!' she said through gritted teeth. 'We've got you the most special present in the world for the most special girl in the world.'

The crowd clapped enthusiastically.

Fandango rose up beside her. He too looked like he'd been in a fearful scrap, his clothes hanging down in shreds, his wig

half hanging off.

In his arms was a beast about the size of a large teddy bear. It was a dopey-looking critter with a crazily long nose, a bit like a giant armadillo or anteater, but with blue fur and huge liquid brown eyes.

Along the ridge of its back were a series of wobbly, rather ridiculous-looking nodules.

'Are you kidding me?' Gertrude said slowly. 'Are you seriously saying that is a *dinosaur?*'

The odd creature scanned the crowd with a bewildered expression.

Then it let out a long and noxious fart.

Hidden amongst the presents, the squirrels shook with laughter.

'Farty fart face!' Alfie whispered. 'Alfie loves the farty dinysaur!'

The room filled with the vilest possible stench of rotting eggs. Some of the adults put handkerchiefs to their mouths. The Duke gagged.

'Oh my goodness!' Rosalba pinched her nose.

Rosalba and Fandango clambered hastily out of the Pop-O-Matic.

The Duchess reached into her handbag and pulled out a perfume bottle. She squirted the flowery scent over the stinky creature.

It sneezed.

Everything went quiet as the birthday girl stepped forward …

CHAPTER 6

UNGRATEFUL GERTRUDE

Gertrude examined her gift. She prised open the creature's mouth, revealing a set of bright pink gums and a leathery green tongue.

'Where are its teeth?' she asked. Her mouth twisted into an angry pout.

'Well,' Fandango stammered, 'it's more of a slime eater. I don't think it's actually got—'

'*Slime eater?*' the birthday girl snapped. 'My father, the Duke of *Appleton*, paid you a *fortune* to go back in time and get me a dinosaur for my ninth birthday, and you come back with a farting, blue, slime-eating *smurf?*'

Over in their hiding place, the squirrels had to work hard not to giggle. Alfie was the worst, stuffing his hand into his mouth to try not to laugh.

The Duke stepped forward. His face had become quite pale. He stroked his daughter's hair, but she swatted his hand away.

'It's got quite big claws, sweetness,' he said nervously.

Gertrude examined the creature's feet.

'I've seen bigger claws on a hamster,' she declared.

'You're the only girl in the world who's got a real dinosaur,' her mother said soothingly. 'You should be grateful!'

'She should,' Ben whispered to his friends amongst the gifts. 'I'd give anything to have my own dinosaur.'

Tears flooded down the little girl's cheeks.

'You don't love me,' she sobbed. 'If you really loved me, you would have got a *proper* dinosaur. This thing is pathetic and I don't want it!'

'It's got lovely big brown eyes,' Rosalba said. 'Don't you think it's the sweetest—'

'Go back in time again!' Gertrude stamped her foot on the floor. 'And get me a *dinosaur*. A massive great big scary one like the ones in the movies.'

'You'd better do as she says,' the Duchess muttered to Rosalba and Fandango. 'Bad

things happen when we don't do as
Gertrude says.'

'*Very* bad things,' Gertrude added,
her eyes narrowing in a sinister fashion.

'I can't do it!' Rosalba declared. She
gestured to her shredded ballgown,
the broken heels on her shoes.

Fandango nodded fervently as he wiped
drippy mud from his hair.

'I agree with her,' he said. 'We were
lucky to survive one journey back in time;
we can't do another.'

'You could *sue* them!' Gertrude
suggested to her father, a sly tone entering
her voice.

The Duke's eyebrows arched upwards.

'Sue them? Capital idea, my sweet
pumpkin. So be it! I will sue you for a
million pounds in damages for ruining my
precious daughter's *life*.'

'*Ruining*,' Gertrude repeated with a sob.
The ballroom went quiet.

'A million?' whispered Salty, drooling as

he thought of the money.

'A million?' gasped Rosalba.

'Well, let's not be too hasty,' Fandango said. 'Maybe we can find a—'

'Get back in that machine,' the Duke said, 'and get my daughter her dinosaur. If you don't fulfil your obligations, I will see you both in court!'

Rosalba and Fandango climbed, very reluctantly, back into the Pop-O-Matic 3000 TT.

Moments later, they were fading from view inside the capsule as the TT convertor kicked in.

Ten minutes passed.

Twenty.

Then came the familiar fizzing and popping sound of the time capsule returning.

'Finally!' Gertrude exclaimed.

The lid of the Pop-O-Matic shot open. The crowd gasped. The children shrank back against the walls. A shaggy and

extremely large blue furry head emerged. Dinner-plate-sized eyes. Flubbery lips. Wobbly nodules on its back the size of windsurfer sails.

Rosalba and Fandango were nowhere to be seen.

Every inch was taken up by the dinosaur.

'Yay!' Gertrude exclaimed, uncertainly.

The creature jumped to the ground. The ballroom floor shook with the weight of it, the crystal shards of the chandeliers tinkling as they swayed. The new arrival looked roughly the same species as the farty blue smurf. But a hundred times bigger.

Twice the size of an elephant.

No, three times!

Gertrude's face went pale. Her knees started to wobble.

Inside the pile of presents, Alfie began to suck his tail.

'Alfie frightened,' he whispered, his fur trembling.

'Don't panic,' the Duke said soothingly.
'The poor thing has obviously come in
search of its child. I'll calm it down with
some food.'

The Duke picked up a dish of Cheesy
Wotsits. He slowly walked across the
ballroom, the cheesy snacks dancing
around in the bowl as his hand trembled.

The massive creature scowled.

A threatening growl started deep in its
throat.

CHAPTER 7

BAGUETTE OBLIVION

'Nice kitty,' the Duke said, his voice rather squeaky. 'Look what I've got for you. Some lovely—'

'**RAAAARGH!**'

The creature roared as it smashed a dustbin-sized fist down on the table. Gertrude's birthday cake was annihilated in a flurry of flying cream and splattered sponge.

The children screamed as their party clothes got peppered with flying food.

'**RAAAARGH!**' The creature roared again. It squelched a raspberry jelly into a thousand slimy globules with another blow of its fist.

'Ah!' The Duke jumped back. Jelly was dripping from his chin, the walls, the chandeliers. The Cheesy Wotsits cascaded from their container.

The creature looked around the room.

'**GLOOGLICK?**' it roared.

Over in the corner, the little critter gave a pathetic answering cry, mewing like a lost kitten. A misty tear ran down its cheek.

Then it called, '**MOOGLICK?**'

The partygoers held their breath.

An unmistakeable expression of pleasure swept the big creature's face.

'**GLOOOOOOGLICK!**' it cried.

The big blue shaggy anteater-type thing shuffled over and sniffed at the little baby.

It snorted, then jumped back. The giant eyes narrowed. The expression of joy soured to something close to anger. A big globule of snot plipped out of its nose and slopped on to the floor.

'**MOOGLICK?**' the little critter mewed.

The big one sniffed again. It sneezed. A deep grumbling snarl began in its belly.

'**MOOGLICK?**' the tiny dinosaur called again, the tone more desperate.

Inside their hiding place, within the pyramid of presents, Cassie turned to the other squirrels.

'The baby smells wrong,' she whispered. 'The Duchess sprayed it with perfume.'

'**RAAAARGH!**' came the reply as the big one shook its head back and forth.

'The mummy's rejecting it,' Ben muttered. 'This could get ugly.'

Everyone in the ballroom held their breath as the big creature glared at the little one, suspicion and confusion in its eyes.

The little dinosaur started to tremble. It jumped into the Duke's arms for protection.

'Get off me!' he yelled.

At that moment, the mother dinosaur got distracted by some of the spilled jelly, lowering its head to sniff.

The Duke retreated, trying to disentangle himself from the whimpering baby creature. On the way he accidentally stood on one of the spilled Cheesy Wotsits which disintegrated with a foamy little **CRUNCH**.

The tiny noise was barely audible, but instantly the big creature's head whipped round.

The Duke froze in position, mid-step, one leg raised in the air.

'**RAAAARGH!**' the big one cried.

Two back feet thumped against the ground, causing the floor to shudder, the chandeliers to wobble overhead.

It stepped towards the Duke, who was trying ever more desperately to rid himself of the baby.

'I said get off me, you stupid … ' the Duke snarled.

But the little one just held on tighter round his neck.

One pace. Two.

The menacing grumble got louder with every moment.

The giant slobbery lips wobbled furiously.

The huge eyes flashed.

'Darling?' the Duchess squeaked. 'It's looking a teensy bit angry. Don't you think you should—'

'I can handle this, sweetie,' the Duke replied.

Using his free hand, the Duke picked up a baguette from the food table.

He pointed it like a sword.

'Don't come any closer,' he said to the dinosaur. 'I'm not afraid to use this, you know—'

'**GRAAAARGH!**'

The creature's front leg whizzed through the air, crunching the French loaf into a million crumbs.

Then it pounced. With surprising speed.

'Whoa!'

The Duke had no time to turn and run.
Instead his reflexes took over and he
jumped upwards, on to the table, then
higher still, grabbing hold of one of the
crystal chandeliers.

The mummy dinosaur swiped.

'Get off me, you beast!' The Duke raised
his legs up to escape the lunging claws of
his attacker, the little dinosaur clutching
for dear life, bleating like a terrified lamb,
as he swung back and forth.

The mummy soared upwards, grabbing
hold of the chandelier.

The squirrels gasped.

Cracks appeared in the ceiling.

'The whole roof's going to come down!'
Cassie hissed.

Alfie wailed and put his paws over his
head.

The three of them swung one way. For a
few crazy seconds they were all hanging on.

CHAPTER 8

THE STINK OF REJECTION

The creature grunted enthusiastically.

'The mummy's enjoying it!' Cassie whispered.

The crazy dinosaur swung harder. The Duke went white in the face. The little one whimpered louder.

'Look out!' screamed the Duchess.

A splintering noise split the air. The chandelier broke away.

The threesome crashed down to earth in a cascade of crystal pieces, ceiling plaster and chalky white dust.

The gifts went flying. The squirrels spilled out in a tumble of tails and fur.

A hundred children, a dozen adults and two rather stressed dinosaurs stared in astonishment.

The Duke shook debris from his hair.
'Squirrels!' yelled the children.
'Squirrels?' the Duke exclaimed.
'Whatever next?'

'**GRAAAARGH!**' roared the mummy dinosaur.

It swatted at the gifts, sending them flying in all directions.

The dinosaur lunged at the squirrels.

'Up the curtains!' Cassie yelled.

The squirrels jumped back, then scampered up the curtains to safety.

The Duke ran back to the other end of the ballroom where the Duchess was gathering the children together.

'Run for your lives!' she exclaimed to the crowd.

The children made a dash for the doorway. In seconds they were out.

The big dinosaur lumbered after them and the ballroom went quiet.

The squirrels climbed back down.

'Phew!' said Cassie.

'That was a close one,' said Ben.

'What a mess,' Salty added. He scooped a generous pawful of cream cake from the floor and slurped it down.

The squirrels gazed at the room, the food spilled everywhere, the presents scattered about. The young dinosaur was sitting in the corner, stuffing sausage rolls into its toothless mouth.

A sudden noise came from beneath the presents. A gurgle, to be precise.

The squirrels pulled the gifts away.

'It's the baby!' Alfie cried.

'They forgot him in the panic!' Cassie said.

They retrieved the cot and smoothed the baby's blankets as he began to stir. The baby smiled with delight as he saw the squirrels.

Salty put his face close.

'Coochee coocheee, wee one,' he said. 'Dinnae fuss about the nasty great dinosaur; we'll protect you.'

The baby's expression changed. The little one screwed up his face and began to cry.

Then the baby blue furry dinosaur did the same.

'This is a disaster,' Ben said. 'That mummy dinosaur has rejected little farty! What can we do to help?'

'Alfie says yes! Help the little dinysaur,' Alfie added.

The squirrels thought for a few moments.

'I know,' Cassie said. 'Why don't we put the baby dino in a shower and get rid of the smell of the perfume?'

'Brilliant!' Ben exclaimed. 'Then it can roll around in its own slime a bit till it stinks like it did when it arrived and the mummy will accept it again and everything will be fine.'

'Yay!' Alfie yelled. 'Alfie loved the farty smurf when it was smelly!'

'You all right to stay here and look after the baby, Salty?' Ben asked. 'We can't leave him here alone.'

'Och aye,' Salty said. 'Nae problem – the wee nipper's in safe hands with old Salty. Off you go and see if you can help

with the dinosaurs, pals, and I'll keep
everything safe as houses here for the wee
babby.'

He patted the infant's head with his
paw. The volume of the baby's cry
increased to a persistent wail.

'Okay,' Cassie said. 'We'll be back as
soon as we can. Come on, Ben, Alfie.'

The three squirrels picked up the little
blue creature and ran out of the ballroom,
heading for the stairway and the upper
floor.

CHAPTER 9

BABY
BOO-BOO

Half an hour later, the squirrels came back to the ballroom where they found Salty playing keepie-up with a scrumpled ball of wrapping paper.

'Twenty-two, twenty-three, twenty-four—'

'Salty?' Ben said.

'Twenty-five, twenty-six, twenty—'

'Salty!' Cassie snapped.

Salty fumbled the ball.

'Now look what you've done,' he moaned.

'Our mission was a success,' Ben told him. 'We washed all the perfume off the little one and the mummy recognised it. The kids are all up there in Gertrude's playroom, taking selfies with the dinosaurs.'

'Great,' Salty said. He scratched vigorously at his backside.

Alfie was looking in the cot.

'Alfie can't see the baby,' he said. 'Where the baby, Salty?'

The squirrels stared around the room.

'Like he said. Where's the baby?' Cassie asked.

Salty shrugged, his expression shifty. 'Baby? What baby?'

Cassie's eyes narrowed. 'The baby you said would be as safe as houses if we left him with you.'

'Oh, *that* baby. Who knows?' he said. 'Baby like that might have crawled anywhere, really.'

'Liccle baby!' Alfie called. 'Liccle baby, where are you?'

No answering cry came back.

'Stop messing about, Salty,' Ben said. 'Where is he?'

Salty shrugged.

'Dunno,' he said.

Cassie and Ben stared at Salty for a few moments.

'*Dunno?*' Cassie cried. 'Are you saying you've *lost* the baby?'

'Och no,' Salty said. 'Not *lost*, exactly. I mean, I think I know where it is.'

'*Think* you know?' Cassie spluttered.

'Och, all right, I just took it for a wee spin in the Pop-O-Matic TT,' Salty said.

He examined his paw closely, picking some fluff out from beneath a claw then scratching at his neck.

'What?' Cassie gasped.

'Well, the babby was screaming and bawling like a little idiot,' Salty said. 'I couldnae get a moment's peace, so I thought it would be a way to entertain the wee bairn.'

'You took that baby back to the time of the dinosaurs?' Cassie asked.

'Aye,' Salty said casually.

Ben raised the lid of the Pop-O-Matic so he could take a look inside.

'So, where is he now?' he said.

'B-b-b-aby g-g-g-one!' Alfie stuttered. 'Alfie scared.'

'Salty?' Cassie moved in close to her friend, her eyes fixed on him with a glare. 'Have you got something to tell us?'

Salty bit his lip.

'Nope,' he said.

'Are you sure?' Ben pressed him. 'Where's the baby?'

'Okay!' Salty spluttered. 'I think I might have accidentally left it behind. I just put it down for a wee second in the jungle and it crawled away. Next thing I knew, pals, there were creepy noises and whatnot all about me so I decided to come back here.'

'Without the baby?' Cassie clutched a paw to her head.

'Aye, it's a real pity,' Salty said with a deep sigh. 'Poor wee bairn all on its own in the time of the dinosaurs.'

He dabbed at his eye. Then he sighed.

'I don't believe this,' Cassie slumped to the floor. 'We trusted you with *one* thing, Salty. One thing! And you've completely messed up!'

'Och well, it'll probably be fine,' Salty continued. 'Chances are it'll be a lot happier there than it was here.'

'Happier?' Ben said. 'Would you be "happier" if you were a snack for a Stegosaurus? A morsel for a Mastodon? A titbit for a Triceratops?'

'There's no choice,' Cassie snapped. 'We've got to go back in time! Rescue the baby before it's too late.'

'But—' Salty gulped.

Cassie gripped Salty by the scruff of the neck.

'We've got to save the baby!' she said.

'Get in,' Ben told him.

Cassie gave Salty a push and he climbed, grumbling loudly, into the Pop-O-Matic 3000 TT as the others joined him.

Cassie activated the switch.

Salty slammed the lid shut with a bad-tempered grunt.

'Yay!' Alfie cried. 'We're going to the time of the dinysaurs!'

65,000,000 YEARS BC
BEWARE OF DINOSAURS!

CHAPTER 10

PRIMEVAL POPPING

The squirrels shivered as the machine began to hum. Neon-green sparks were shooting off the end of their paws and ears.

'Your noses are glowing!' Alfie exclaimed. 'Alfie loves it!'

The view through the glass panel started to shift. The background began to blur, then spin. The metal of the machine became hot to the touch.

'The world's going wiggly!' Alfie exclaimed.

A siren blasted off. The friends covered their ears.

The Pop-O-Matic 3000 TT shuddered.

The squirrels fell in a heap at the bottom.

All went quiet. Then a symphony of new sounds reached the ears of our friends.

The shimmering sound of a million insects on the wing. The drip–drip of moisture on waxy leaves.

Raising the lid of the Pop-O-Matic, the four friends peered out.

At a *fantastical* and primeval world.

The Pop-O-Matic had ended its journey in a steamy rainforest. A rainforest of exotic wonders.

The trees were simply gargantuan, wider than ten trees back home and stretching high enough that the tops seemed to touch the clouds.

Cassie, Ben and Alfie climbed out and began to explore.

Salty stayed by the popcorn machine.

'I've got a wee bit of a tummy ache, pals,' Salty said, peering into the jungle. 'Best I stay here to guard the time machine, eh?'

'We stick together,' Cassie told him. 'Besides, I wouldn't want to be on my own if a Tyrannosaurus Rex happened by.'

Salty swallowed hard as he scanned the dark shadows.

A fruit the size of a dustbin fell off a nearby tree with a mighty crash.

'Aye, well, perhaps you're right,' Salty said. He climbed out to join the others.

'Liccle baby?' Alfie whispered. 'Are you there?'

They pushed through the sprawling bushes and shrubs. On them were flowers, but they were flowers unlike any the squirrels had ever seen. Their colours were luminescent, glowing with internal light.

One bright orange specimen was utterly bizarre. It had lips like a mouth, with teeth etched into the petal.

'That's just a trick, pals,' Salty said. 'Obviously, it can't actually bite.'

He thrust his paw into the weird-looking opening.

SNAP! The plant chomped down, trapping him in an instant.

'Aaaaargh!' Salty cried. 'It's got me!'

The others grabbed him, giggling as the fight became a tug of war.

'Salty's getting eaten by a flower!' Alfie yelled.

Salty's paw popped out, covered in strange yellow goo that resembled custard.

'Yuck!' Salty shook his hand to get rid of the gunk.

The friends took a few more steps then ducked down as a dragonfly whirred past.

A dragonfly the size of a small aeroplane.

'Did you see its eyes?' Cassie gulped. 'Big as footballs.'

A spine-chilling cry split the air. High-pitched like a banshee. The squirrels spun around, staring wide-eyed into the gloom.

'Was that *Rosalba?*' Ben said.

'She and Fandango are still somewhere in this time zone,' Cassie said. 'We'll just have to try and avoid them.'

A furry shape twisted in the shadows.

A vine shivered as something unseen climbed it up high.

Insects droned away, a constant buzz. Then they stopped.

PLIP! A puddle of bubbling mud plopped up nearby. The squirrels jumped.

'Everything is under control,' Cassie said, her voice wobbling a bit. 'We just have to keep our wits about us and everything will be fine.'

'Oh aye,' Salty spluttered. 'We're only lost in the time of the dinosaurs and probably about to get eaten alive by a starving pack of Velociraptors.'

'Yay!' Alfie shouted. 'Alfie wants to meet the Veloci-whatsits as well!'

'Don't be negative,' Ben said to Salty. 'We need to be positive if we're going to find that baby.'

'Besides, it's your fault all this has happened in the first place,' Cassie said. 'You should be grateful we're here to try and put things right.'

'That's right,' Salty moaned. 'Always old Salty's fault, isn't it? Go on, blame me, I'm used to it.'

Cassie held up her paw.

'Shhhh!' she said.

The friends were silent. In the distance they heard the noise of a baby laughing.

CHAPTER 11

VOLCANIC RUMBLINGS

'I think that's the baby!' Cassie said. 'Let's head in that direction.'

Salty stayed put for a few moments, then turned back in the direction of the Pop-O-Matic.

'I've gone far enough,' he said. 'I'm staying with the machine, and that's final!'

'Go on, then,' Cassie said. 'We'll see you later.'

Salty soon vanished, following the tracks they had made on the muddy floor.

Cassie led the way through the jungle, the humid air thick with the rich aroma of rotting vegetation and peaty soil.

It was a super-tangled obstacle course. Fallen trees to clamber over. Sticky spider webs to push through. Huge yellow and

black stripy flowers in the shape of super-sized wasps, dripping green slime on their heads.

Parting the fronds revealed a sinister sight ahead. A jet-black mountain in the shape of a perfect cone.

Huge creatures flapped around the slopes on leathery wings. A sickly plume of yellow smoke trickled from the top.

'A smoky mountain,' Alfie said, his eyes shining with pleasure. 'Alfie wants to climb it.'

Cassie put her paw on Alfie's shoulder. 'A smoky mountain, Alfie,' she said, 'is a *volcano.*'

'Yay! Alfie *loves* volcanoes,' Alfie said. 'Is it going to go bang? Alfie wants to see it go BANG!'

'Let's not think about that,' Cassie said. 'Let's think about saving that baby.'

The cooing noise came again. The faraway sound of a baby having a lot of fun.

They climbed up a slope and pushed through a final thicket.

'Little baby!' Ben called. 'Are you there?'

There was no reply, and now the landscape had changed. It was suddenly more open. They were walking across a field of high grasses and other plants which looked strangely familiar even though they were ten times bigger than anything they had ever seen before.

'These grains look like popcorn kernels,' Ben said.

Cassie touched one of the rugby-ball-sized pods.

'It's wild corn,' she said. 'Supersized.'

'Imagine if we could pop it!' Ben said.

Alfie gasped. 'The biggest ever popcorn in the whole wiggly world!'

The squirrels licked their lips as they thought about that treat. Then Cassie looked up and frowned.

'Look at the sky,' she said. 'There are two suns.'

The squirrels looked up. Cassie was right. The sun was blazing in one part of the sky, and a smaller bright light was glowing nearby.

'I don't think it's a second sun,' Cassie said with a nervous shrug. 'Maybe it's a comet or something.'

'Or an asteroid,' Ben said. He frowned. 'You know the thing about the dinosaurs being made extinct by a giant asteroid smashing into the earth? You don't suppose we've time-travelled back to the deadly moment … do you?'

'Shhh!' Cassie held up her hand. 'What's that strange smell?'

The stench of rotten eggs filled the air. The squirrels sniffed.

'It's coming from the volcano,' Ben said. He pointed once more to the peak, where the plume of sulphurous gas was thicker than before.

The squirrels continued and soon reached the river.

'We're getting close!' Cassie hissed. They heard the baby gurgling happily in the forest on the far side of the water.

'Wheeeeeee!'

Followed by a splat.

Then,

'Wheeeeeee!'

Then another splat.

'That's the baby,' Cassie said eagerly. 'Let's go.'

The squirrels splashed across the river and, ever alert to danger, followed the sound.

CHAPTER 12

SULPHUROUS STINK

Good news and bad news awaited Cassie, Ben and Alfie.

The good news was they did indeed find the baby.

The bad news was that the baby had a new chum.

The baby had befriended a young dinosaur, a juvenile about the size of a minibus with a graceful long neck and a tiny head.

'What species is that, Ben?' Cassie asked. 'We all know you're a bit of a dinosaur nut!'

'I think it's an Alamosaurus,' Ben whispered.

'What if it wants to eat the b-b-b-baby?' Alfie stammered.

'It's a herbivore,' Ben said. 'Only eats plants.'

SPLAT!

The baby and his new friend were playing in a wallow of gloopy mud which had covered the baby.

'That baby is an adrenaline junkie,' Cassie muttered.

'Can Alfie play?' Alfie begged.

Cassie eyed the Alamosaurus's feet, each one big enough to squash a squirrel flat in a second. Then she saw the tail, as thick as a tree trunk, easily strong enough to swipe a small furry mammal into oblivion if the creature was provoked.

'No!' Cassie told him. 'We don't know how that creature will react if it knows we're here. We have to wait until it gets bored, then we can make a grab for the baby.'

The squirrels settled down to watch, finding that the baby and his new friend had come up with an inventive game. First, the Alamosaurus lowered its mighty head so the baby could clamber on top. Then, uttering a happy 'Wheeee!', the baby used the dinosaur's neck as a slide, whizzing down at high speed and flying off the end to land in

the mud pool with a satisfying

The game went on. And on. And on.

The baby was tireless and so was his new friend.

After half an hour, Ben was getting itchy.

'We need to get back to the time machine soon,' he said. 'Don't forget that Rosalba and Fandango are here in this time zone as well, and we can't let them leave us stranded.'

'All right,' Cassie agreed. 'One more slide and we'll try and snatch the baby.'

The baby splashed down in the gloop.

The squirrels rushed forward, sending droplets of slime flying.

'Grab him!' Ben cried.

The three friends reached for the baby.

But the mud was too slippery and trying
to grip him was like trying to hold on to
a wet bar of soap in the bath.

'Googoo,' the baby laughed. He thought
it was a game.

But the Alamosaurus was less impressed.
'**GROAAAR!**' it roared.

The dinosaur bent forward and snatched
the baby up by the nappy. Then it turned,
with the baby held in its mouth.

'Don't let it get away!' Cassie yelled.

The giant herbivore hurried off with
a surprising turn of speed. The squirrels
gave chase.

Pushing through the thick vegetation.

Diving into the river.

Then across the grassy zone where the
giant corn plants swayed in the breeze.

The herbivore paced towards some
cliffs, where a dark area of shadow could
be seen.

'It's heading for that cave,' Ben said.

The Alamosaurus kept moving.

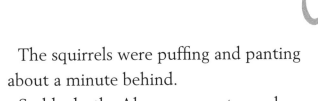

The squirrels were puffing and panting about a minute behind.

Suddenly, the Alamosaurus stopped. It stared at the opening to the cave and gave a great shudder.

The snake-like neck came down.

The baby rolled free.

The dinosaur spun around, and ran towards nearby woods.

'Something frightened it,' Cassie said.

The baby kept on crawling towards the cave. Cassie and the friends followed.

Then the squirrels saw something that made their fur prickle.

In front of the cave was a clearing.

'Uh oh,' Cassie exclaimed. 'Now I understand why that herbivore did a runner.'

The squirrels ducked behind a boulder, catching their breath as they sneaked a look ahead.

Lying in the clearing was a large group of sleeping dinosaurs. Even at rest they

were a terrifying sight, each one a finely
tuned killing machine, muscles bulging
behind greeny-brown lizard-like shiny
skin.

They were a similar shape to a
Tyrannosaurus Rex, but much smaller.

The pack had been hunting. Littered
around the clearing were the carcasses
of prey. Huge creatures. Bones picked as
clean as ivory tusks.

'Velociraptors!' Ben exclaimed. 'The
fastest and most dangerous predators of
all. They hunt in packs.'

The baby crawled right up to the biggest
of the creatures.

'Oh no,' Cassie whispered. 'I'm
beginning to get a bad feeling about this.'

CHAPTER 13

SLIPPERY CUSTOMER

The baby tickled the sleeping dinosaur on the nose.

'Silly baby!' Ben muttered. 'It's going to wake up.'

The predator stirred. The eyes remained shut.

The baby giggled. Then he slapped the creature. Hard.

The Velociraptor wriggled its nose, then yawned wide, revealing a fearsome array of razor-sharp teeth.

The baby stuck his head inside for a few moments, gazing in wonder at the shiny white fangs.

'Googoogoo,' he gurgled softly.

The squirrels clutched at each other, hardly daring to breathe.

'I can't watch,' Ben muttered.

He put his paws over his eyes, then peeked out through a tiny crack.

The baby scraped a handful of slime from the creature's tongue and put it in his mouth.

'Yeeeeurgh!' Cassie whispered.

'Yummy slime!' Alfie giggled.

The baby smacked his lips. He smiled and tasted some more of the slime.

Then he got bored and pulled himself back.

In the nick of time.

SNAP! The dinosaur's jaw clamped shut.

'Phew!' Ben said.

The baby looked around, focussing on the cave entrance for the first time.

'Oooooooh,' he gurgled.

The child crawled on, clambering over one sleeping creature's neck then doing a detour around another before disappearing into the dark cavity of the cave.

'We've got to sneak across and rescue him,' Cassie said. 'But, if there are Velociraptors *outside* that cave, goodness knows what's *inside* it.'

'If we're really quiet, we might make it,' Ben agreed.

The squirrels tiptoed out from behind the boulder, on to the edge of the clearing.

Then,

Crack!

Alfie stepped on a twig.

'Oooops,' Alfie whispered.

One of the dinosaurs stirred. Then another.

The squirrels dashed to cover, peeking back at the clearing.

One by one the dinosaurs shook themselves.

One by one they stood.

The pack was awake.

The biggest of the Velociraptors crossed to the carcasses. It cracked a massive bone between its jaws, crunching the fragments

as easily as a child crunches a crisp.

A snarling, snapping, fight began, the two creatures lunging and biting at each other with terrifying speed and power. Others joined in, growling aggressively.

'They look hungry,' Ben said.

Cassie frowned as thoughts ran through her mind.

'We need to find a way to lure them away,' she said. 'Let's get back to Salty. I've got an idea.'

Back at the Pop-O-Matic 3000 TT, a most bizarre sight was awaiting our squirrel friends.

They had expected to find Salty hiding in the time machine.

But no. Salty was out and about and he had an *audience*.

He was sitting cross-legged on the forest floor, talking away happily.

'Aye, well, it was just after dawn that the weasels came up over the ridge. That's why they call it "the battle of Weasel Ridge", you see, pals, because it was a whole army of savage weasels and they were coming over the top of this ridge … '

Sitting in front of him, lined up neatly like schoolchildren in class, were a dozen cute-looking dinosaur babies. Each the size of a suitcase, they looked like armoured pigs with strangely thin heads and two horns sticking out.

In their eyes there was no sharp flicker of intelligence. Just a dull milky sheen.

They stared adoringly as Salty lectured, continuing his tale with dramatic arm movements.

'All the other squirrels had run away. The weasels had got 'em frit. But not old Salty, oh no, not me, pals. Salty stood his ground as the weasels swarmed over. Thousands of 'em, there were. I waited until I could see the whites of their eyes, pals, the whites of their evil, bloodthirsty, beady eyes, then—'

'Salty?' Cassie said.

Salty stopped in mid flow, spinning round as he heard the others approach.

'Oh, hi pals,' he said. 'Just telling my new chums the story of the battle of Weasel—'

'Yes, we heard,' Ben said.

The three new arrivals stared at the curious critters.

'What are they?' Cassie asked.

CHAPTER 14

CHUBBY
CHUMS

'Leptoceratops,' Ben said, patting one affectionately on the neck. 'One of the smallest herbivore dinosaurs.'

'They don't look very bright,' Cassie said.

'Aye, well,' Salty agreed, 'they're not over-blessed in the brain department. But they *are* great listeners.'

'Alfie loves them,' cried Alfie. He kissed one of the creatures on the nose.

'What about the baby? How's the wee nipper doing?' Salty asked.

'He's gone into a cave,' Cassie explained. 'And there's a whole load of dinosaurs milling around outside it.'

'That doesn't sound too bad,' Salty said. 'All this nonsense about dinosaurs being scary is hogwash!'

He gestured to the baby herbivores.

'Look at them! Sweet as cherry pie! Salty isn't scared of any dinosaur, I can tell you that, pals.'

'That's good, Salty,' Cassie said. 'Because I've got a mission for you.'

Salty puffed out his chest.

'Salty's ready for anything,' he said. 'I fear no man. I fear no creature. I fear nothing but fear itself. And even *that* doesn't scare old Salty.'

'The plan is this,' Cassie said. 'We need to lure those dinosaurs away from the cave, so one of us will have to be bait. We can tie the volunteer to a tree. Draw the dinosaurs in this direction so a couple of us can dash into the cave and save the baby.'

'Yay!' Alfie said. 'Alfie wants to be the bait! Please let Alfie!'

'No, Alfie,' Ben said. 'There's only one squirrel who's a tempting enough snack.'

He paused for a moment before

finishing his statement. 'And that's Salty.'

Salty blinked.

'Did you say *snack*?' His ears twitched.

Cassie winked secretly at Ben.

'He's right,' Cassie said. 'They'll need to get their teeth into something chunky.'

'Chunky?' Salty snorted. 'Who are you calling chunky?'

He gestured to his substantial belly, slapping it with his paw.

'This is muscle, this is, pals – 100 per cent Scottish beefcake!'

'Wibble-wobble belly!' Alfie laughed, wobbling Salty's gut with his little paws. 'Salty got a wibble gut.'

Salty swiped Alfie away.

'Think again, pals,' he said. 'You're not tying old Salty up to be eaten, I'll tell you that.'

'Surely you're not afraid, are you, Salty?' Cassie said. 'Surely the hero of the battle of Weasel Ridge isn't scared of a few silly dinosaurs?'

Salty licked his finger and smoothed his eyebrows.

'Aye, well,' he said, 'that was a battle, that was. If it hadn't been for old Salty, those weasels would have taken over the world.'

'Not many squirrels have got your courage,' Cassie said.

'Or your special forces skills,' Ben added.

Salty nodded. 'That's true,' he said. 'My years in the Squirrel Attack Squadron have turned me into a finely tuned fighting machine. A steely-eyed assassin, a squirrel without fear, a squirrel that—'

'You're my hero, Salty,' Alfie said, his eyes going moist as he stared adoringly up. 'Salty's my hero. And he's going to be my daddy.'

'You can get *that* out of your wee head for starters,' Salty snapped.

Cassie found some emergency supplies stored in a special compartment in the Pop-O-Matic.

She pulled out a length of rope, and she and Ben led the way back towards the cave, getting as close as they dared to the Velociraptors.

'It's time to get you tied up,' she told Salty.

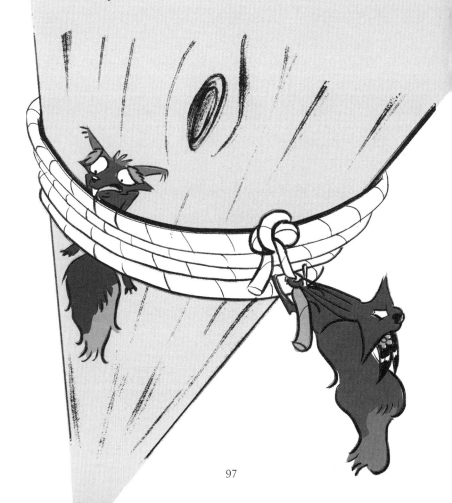

They selected a tree and positioned Salty with his back to it. The rope whizzed round and round as his arms and legs were pinned back.

'Now, just a moment, my old pals,' Salty said. 'I'm clear on the first part of the plan. My scent draws those dinosaurs away from the cave.'

Cassie pulled tight on the rope. 'That's right, Salty,' she said.

'So … er … how many do you think there might be?'

'Oooh, I think we saw about twenty,' Ben said.

'Twenty?' Salty's lower lip started to wobble. 'And, er, what type of dinosaurs did you say they were again?'

'Velociraptors,' Cassie said.

She gave the rope another yank, sealing Salty's belly to the tree.

Salty's eyes widened.

'*Velociraptors?*'

CHAPTER 15

TOOTHY TERROR

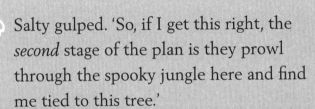

Salty gulped. 'So, if I get this right, the *second* stage of the plan is they prowl through the spooky jungle here and find me tied to this tree.'

Ben added another loop to Salty's legs. 'Exactly, Salty.'

Drops of sweat collected on Salty's ears.

'So … er … old Salty was just wondering … er … what happens next?'

'It's not a problem,' Ben said soothingly. 'Velociraptors hunt on movement. As long as you keep absolutely still, you'll be fine.'

Salty's eyes began to bulge.

'That's the *plan*?' he snorted. 'Old Salty has to keep still as a statue with a hundred ravenous Velociraptors sniffing at his kneecaps? What about my *fleas*, pals, what about my *fleas*?'

'Salty got fleas!' Alfie yelled. 'Fleabag Salty! Fleabag Salty!'

'I thought you said you *didn't* have fleas,' Cassie said.

'Aye, well, I might have a couple, pals, needing a wee bit of scratching from time to time.'

Salty moved his head so he could scratch his ear against the bark of the tree.

Another knot was tied on the rope.

'You'll just have to ignore them,' Ben said.

'Now hang on just a minute, pals,' Salty spluttered. 'I'm having a wee bit of a rethink on this great plan.'

RAAAAARGH!

A mighty growl came from the direction of the cave.

'Too late,' Cassie said.

Another spine-chilling cry echoed across

the valley. Then several more.

'I think the Velociraptors have smelled you,' Ben whispered.

Salty strained at the ropes.

'Wait!' he hissed. 'Pals?'

He scratched his backside rapidly against the tree.

Ben, Cassie and Alfie scampered into the undergrowth as the sound of crunching dinosaur footsteps filled the forest.

Back near the cave, the three friends parted the rubbery leaves.

The entrance to the cave was as dark as the eye socket of a midnight skull, creepers and vines falling down from above like stray hairs.

The route was clear. Not a Velociraptor in sight.

Just the scattered bones of long-dead creatures, the carcasses picked clean.

'Shhhhh!' Cassie whispered.

Coming from deep inside the cave they heard a faint cry.

'Googeegoogoo.'

The gurgle of the baby.

The squirrels crept across the clearing and stood in the gaping entrance.

'Little baby?' Cassie hissed. 'Are you there?'

No reply came back. Just the drip–drip–drip of water droplets raining down from the roof.

'Follow me,' Cassie said.

The squirrels walked into the cave, blinking as their eyes adjusted to the darkness.

They couldn't see much. The shadows were deep.

'Alfie getting a bit scared,' Alfie squeaked.

He clung on to Cassie's paw as they continued down the passage.

Suddenly, a high-pitched whistle echoed off the walls.

Shapes unfolded from the roof of the cave.

The friends ducked down as huge papery wings brushed past. They were hit by a blast of air.

The squirrels froze. More whistles sounded. More rustles as unseen wings beat the air.

'What was that?' Ben said.

Another of the beasts flapped past.

The squirrels got a glimpse of a dog-sized flying creature.

Wings as long as a man.

A furry face with sharp white teeth and a snubby black nose.

'Giant bats!' Cassie exclaimed.

Alfie danced a little jig.

'Alfie loves giant bats,' he said. 'Alfie wants to play with the giant bats!'

Then the squirrels saw a terrible sight.

The baby, clutched in the claws of a bat.

'It's got the baby!' Ben said. 'What can we do now?'

The bat flew towards the light, the baby still clutched beneath it, gurgling happily.

'We'll have to follow,' Cassie said. 'Quick as we can.'

The three friends ran back to the entrance to the cave.

In the forest, Salty was attracting plenty of interest. His richly aromatic scent had drawn all the Velociraptors to investigate.

First he saw their eyes, glinting amongst the dripping leaves of the jungle.

They were eyes without mercy. Cold. Calculating. Killers' eyes.

'Ooooooh, Mammy,' he murmured.

Salty gulped. His tufty ears started to drip with sweat. He strained at the ropes, but they wouldn't budge.

The Velociraptors came closer …

CHAPTER 16

FLEA-BITE FIXATIONS

One by one the Velociraptors crept from the cover of the surrounding jungle, until Salty was surrounded by twenty of the savage-looking predators.

They snuffled amongst the fallen leaves, hunting for scent.

Salty felt an unbearable itching on his neck. His fleas began to bite.

A particularly large Velociraptor came pacing stealthily forward.

A bright glint shone in its eyes.

'Uh oh,' Salty muttered so quietly it was barely louder than breathing. Globules of sweat trickled down his cheeks.

Closer it came. A drip of drool fell from a mouth that was slightly agape, packed with the sharpest teeth Salty had ever seen in his life.

Salty felt his heart pounding so hard he was sure the creature would hear it.

The dinosaur sniffed at Salty's feet.

Salty went rigid. He didn't dare breathe.

The creature growled suspiciously.

It sniffed again, deeper, more prolonged.

A second Velociraptor came close.

Salty kept as still as a statue.

A flea bit into Salty's cheek.

A third Velociraptor took an interest.

Then Salty's situation took an even darker turn.

A flea walked out on to the end of Salty's nose and began to dance a little jig.

Salty went cross-eyed, staring at it in horror.

One of the dinosaurs spotted the movement of Salty's eyes.

It pushed right up close, eyes locked on the hapless squirrel.

The flea jumped up and down.

Salty wrinkled his nose.

The three dinosaurs saw the twitch. Instantly they were more alert, pushing in even closer, until the three heads were just a squirrel's length from Salty's petrified face.

Foul-smelling green dribble began to ooze from their jaws.

Salty's nose trembled. The flea continued to jig around.

One of the Velociraptors licked its lips.

Salty felt the biggest sneeze of his life building up.

A snake-like Velociraptor tongue emerged, dark green and slippery, a good metre long, quivering as it licked Salty on the chin.

The flea chomped down on Salty's nose.

'*AIIICHOOO!*' Salty sneezed.

The three dinosaurs reared back in surprise. Then, as one, an evil grin crossed their faces as they prepared to strike, mouths wide open, eyes filled with the lust for squirrel meat.

Salty screamed.

Then came a voice. Close by in the forest. A woman's voice. Angry. Scolding. Sharp as a finely honed blade.

The Velociraptors froze to the spot.

'Don't talk rubbish, Fandango! It certainly IS your fault,' Rosalba said. 'If you hadn't had your stupid time-travelling fixation, everything would be fine!'

Fandango and Rosalba burst through the trees.

The Velociraptors spun round.

'There's a squirrel tied to that tree!' cried Fandango.

'Never mind the squirrel!' Rosalba screamed. 'It's the dinosaurs, you dummy!'

The Velociraptors began to growl with anticipation. There was a lot more meat on this new prey.

One of the beasts lunged forward.

Rosalba jumped like a startled gazelle, scrabbling up a handy tree, her high-heeled shoes spilling off in the desperate ascent. Fandango was not so quick; he stumbled and fell as the dinosaurs turned.

'Mummy!' he yelled.

The eccentric inventor jumped to his feet and sprinted into the jungle, the pack of Velociraptors in hot pursuit.

CHAPTER 17

SALTY FIGHTS BACK (IN HIS MIND!)

Moments later, the bushes parted again.

Ben, Cassie and Alfie emerged.

'Everything all right?' Ben asked.

Salty scowled.

'Oh aye, never been better,' he said bitterly. 'Facing off against a pack of voracious Velociraptors is my favourite pastime on a Sunday afternoon, pals.'

Cassie and Ben untied the rope.

'Act as a decoy, they said,' Salty muttered. 'Draw them away from the cave, they said. Everything will be fine, they said; you'll only get chomped to pieces by the *evil dinosaur monsters*.'

As soon as he was free he scratched at his nose.

'Don't be fed up, Salty,' Cassie said, patting him on the back. 'You were the one for that job.'

'Only a special-forces legend could win against the most dangerous predator that ever walked the earth,' Ben added.

'You're my all-time-ever hero, Salty!' Alfie cried.

Salty paused, scratching at a flea bite on his rump as he considered his friends' words.

'Aye, well, mebbe you're right,' he said grudgingly. 'There's not many squirrels could fight off 150 hungry Velociraptors with their hands tied behind their *backs*, pals, I'll tell you *that*!'

Salty began to shadow-box, jabbing at the air, his paws clenched into fists.

'They were no match for old Salty,' he proclaimed. 'I sent them packing with their tails between their legs. They won't forget the day they picked a fight with *me*, pals, and that's for sure!'

A sudden rustling came from the tree
above. A dark shape moved.

'A hundred and fifty Velociraptors?'
came a sharp woman's voice.
'I counted about *twenty*.'
'Rosalba?' Cassie called up.
A skinny leg dangled
down. Then another,
followed by the

dishevelled shape
of the former
actress and
popcorn-
manufacturing
businesswoman
herself.

CRASH!

Rosalba slumped to the leafy forest floor and fixed the squirrels with a sour look.

'What are you scabby critters *doing* here?' she snapped, hitching her faded velvet ballgown into place. 'Is there *anywhere* you don't turn up like bad pennies?'

'We're looking for the Appleton baby,' Ben told her. 'Have you seen him?'

'A baby? Who cares about a snotty baby?' Rosalba snorted. 'It's me you should be worried about. *Me!* Rosalba! A world-famous and much-loved former actress stranded and helpless in the time of the savage dinosaurs.'

'Why didn't you come back with the mummy dinosaur in the Pop-O-Matic?' Ben asked.

'It was a disaster!' Rosalba sobbed into a stained silk handkerchief. 'Fandango stuffed the horrible creature on to the seats and that giant bottom nudged the controls! Of all the rotten luck! The time machine started up and before we could stop it – PUFF! – it was gone.'

Rosalba pointed to the sky.

'And now there's a massive asteroid about to obliterate the planet.'

The squirrels looked up. To that curiously bright light, almost like a second sun, which now seemed even brighter than before.

Ben and Cassie shared a worried look.

'My suspicion was right,' Ben murmured.

'It does look even closer now,' Cassie whispered.

'We're doomed!' Rosalba wailed. 'Doomed, I tell you.'

Alfie stared at the deadly ball of fire.

'Alfie likes the shiny thing!' he exclaimed, dancing a little jig. 'It's pretty!'

CHAPTER 18

NEMESIS

'Pretty?' Rosalba exclaimed. 'You'll see how *pretty* it is soon enough, you flea-bitten idiot. Fandango told me all about it. It's an asteroid made of rock and iron, eight miles wide. It's shooting through space faster than a speeding bullet and in a very short time indeed it will smash into that volcano over there and create mayhem across the entire world, obliterating virtually all life, ending the dinosaur era and boiling the oceans dry.'

Salty poked his finger at Rosalba.

'Asteroids?' Salty scoffed, his eyes bulging with indignation. 'Salty's not frit of any old stupid *asteroids*, lady. My old gran up in Glasgow had an attack of *asteroids*, and she got rid of them with a wee bitty bit of cream on her backside, so don't try and frighten old Salty with

scare stories about *asteroids*! Pah!'

Cassie and Ben shared a worried look.

'We've got to find that baby and get out of here,' Cassie whispered. 'There's not a moment to lose.'

Ben nodded. Then he cocked his head as a distant 'gooing' noise came on the wind.

A gurgle in the distance.

'The baby!' Ben exclaimed. 'Cassie, come with me; everyone else, stay here.'

Rosalba scowled.

'Where's the Pop-O-Matic?' she blurted. 'Take me to it, quickly!'

Cassie whispered to Salty. 'Don't show her, Salty. It's vital she doesn't get to that machine. She'll zap off on her own and leave us all here.'

Salty nodded wisely.

'Oh aye,' he replied with a knowing wink, 'you can depend on old Salty. One hundred per cent. I won't spill the beans, no sir, no matter what tricks she may pull; old Salty will *never* reveal the location of the Pop-O-Matic. Ever.'

Cassie looked at Rosalba, her eyes filled with doubt.

The baby gurgled again. Fainter this time.

'Come on!' Ben cried.

Ben grabbed Cassie by the hand and they vanished into the jungle.

Alfie snuggled up close to the actress, gazing up, his eyes full of hope.

'Will you be my mummy?' he pleaded.

The elderly actress shuddered in horror. 'Certainly not!' she fired back. 'Not in this – or any other – time zone.'

Rosalba located her high-heeled shoes, scraping mud from the fabric and pulling them on with some difficulty.

'So, brave squirrel, where is the Pop-O-Matic TT?' she asked Salty.

Salty laughed.

'Och, you cannae catch old Salty out that easy, lady. I've got my orders and I'm following them!'

Rosalba smiled, her mouth twisting into a sly grimace.

'What a shame!' she murmured. 'When I'm just bursting to tell someone about what I've seen in the jungle here. The solid gold fruit of the diddlydiddly dumdum tree.'

Salty's eye twitched.

'Solid gold?' he said, suspiciously. 'Diddlydiddly dumdum tree?'

'Oh yes,' Rosalba said casually, examining her nails in a leisurely fashion. 'Worth *millions* if only there was someone strong enough and clever enough to harvest it. There for the taking. A kilo of solid eighteen-carat gold in every fruit.'

'A kilo? Solid gold?' Salty repeated. A glazed look came over his eyes.

'Indeed!' the actress added. 'And it's ripe for the taking; the dinosaurs don't care about money. Just think, millions of pounds of shiny gold bullion, just waiting to be plucked from the branches by an

eager hand. Or paw.'

A sticky drop of drool plopped out of the corner of Salty's mouth.

'Treasure!' Salty said, dreamily. 'Real treasure for old Salty. Tell me more, dear lady, tell me more.'

CHAPTER 19

GOLDEN DREAMS

'We'll have to split it, fifty–fifty. Partners.'
Rosalba added.

'Yes, yes. Whatever you say. Now, w-w-
w-where is it?' Salty stammered. 'Salty's
the squirrel to harvest the diddlydiddly
dumdum tree! Which direction is it? Tell
old Salty! NOW, this moment! I'll be rich!
A millionaire at last!'

'Yay! Money from the diddlydum trees!'
Alfie sang. He danced around Salty in
sheer delight.

'Not so fast,' Rosalba said. Her spidery
eyelashes fluttered at high speed and she
leaned towards Salty as her voice became
low and husky. 'First we need to check
how *many* kilos of gold we can stash
in the Pop-O-Matic. It might be thirty.

It could be fifty. Let's go and see how wealthy we are going to become, shall we, once we harvest the incredible riches of the diddlydiddly dumdum tree?'

Salty spun around eagerly, leading Rosalba into the jungle.

'This way, lady,' he said. 'Let's not waste a second.'

Salty sang a little tune as he tramped through the vegetation.

'Millions for me
Millions for me
Millions for me
From the diddlydiddly … er, what was the next bit again?'

'Dumdum tree,' Rosalba said with a smirk.

'Oh aye, dumdum tree.'

It took just a few minutes to find the Pop-O-Matic 3000 TT in the little clearing. Rosalba's eyes shone hungrily as she saw it.

'Excellent,' Rosalba said smoothly. She

rubbed her hands. 'I'll just pop in and see about the storage space.'

'Go ahead,' Salty exclaimed enthusiastically, gesturing to the giant machine. 'Be my guest! It'll be a pleasure to see how much treasure we can take!'

A chipped scarlet fingernail pressed against a metal catch. The great glass lid popped open with a hiss of compressed air.

'Give me a hand to move this log,' the actress said. 'I need a step up.'

'Aye,' Salty agreed. 'Whatever the lady wants, the lady gets.'

Salty and Alfie helped Rosalba to place an old trunk in position. She clambered in with a grunt.

'It looks most encouraging,' she called from the interior. 'I reckon we could fit about eighty kilos of gold in here.'

Salty jumped up and down with glee. He slapped a high five with Alfie.

'Eighty? D'you hear that, little pal? Eighty kilos! I'll build a solid gold statue

126

of old Salty on the summit of Ben Nevis, fifty metres high! And popcorn for life!'

'Alfie wants his own popcorn machine!' Alfie cried.

'You will have one, my little pal, you will,' Salty said generously, patting the little squirrel on the head.

Rosalba told them from the interior, 'I'll just check the lid will close okay.'

'Good plan,' Salty replied, trying to suppress his laughter as he thought of the riches that would soon be his.

The lid snapped shut. Salty and Alfie had to lean in close to hear Rosalba's final muffled words through the glass.

'I'll just make sure the dials are working okay,' the cunning actress called.

'Righto!' Salty agreed, smiling broadly.

Lights began to flash. The machine shuddered.

'W-w-w-what's happening?' Salty stuttered.

'So long, suckers!' Rosalba cried, her voice

muffled but ecstatic. 'You're all doomed!
Doomed, I tell you! Doomed to be fried
to a crisp by the killer asteroid, along with
all the rest of life on earth.'

'What?' Salty said. 'What do you mea—'

Rosalba slammed a lever down.

'Erm, now hang on just a—' Salty gasped.

The Pop-O-Matic 3000 TT shimmered for a few moments, an electronic hum coming from deep within. Then came the pink smoke. Then the green.

PLIZZZZZZZ!

It was gone.

'Yay!' Alfie cried. 'Alfie loves it when the machine goes whizz … bang … gone!'

'Hmmm,' Salty declared. He rolled the log with his foot, as if the machine might be somehow hiding beneath it. He scratched his head and picked out a flea as the clear light of realisation flickered into his eyes. 'But … erm … ' He frowned. 'Ah. Oops!'

CHAPTER 20

LOSING TIME

Ben and Cassie stared at the empty space where the Pop-O-Matic 3000 TT had been standing.

Cassie's mouth fell open as she saw the smoke lingering in the tropical air.

'Where's the time machine?' Ben squeaked. 'What have you done with it?'

Salty gulped, stepping backwards as his eyes rolled.

'T-t-t-time machine?' he stammered. 'What time machine would that be, pals?'

Cassie took a firm stride towards Salty, her eyes glimmering.

'And where is Rosalba?' she snapped.

'She whizzed off!' Alfie sang out. 'Salty got tricked! Yay!'

'Salty!' Ben hissed. 'You didn't let

Rosalba escape, did you?'

'You *idiot*!' Cassie barked, her voice brittle with anger.

Ben and Cassie took another pace towards Salty. He retreated, falling backwards on the tree stump and scrabbling along the earthy floor.

'Now, hang on just a minute, pals,' Salty gasped. 'She hypnotised me with her spooky eyes. My brain went all fuzzy. I was under her evil spell!'

'Your brain's ALWAYS fuzzy!' Ben cried.

Cassie sat down heavily, her head cradled in her paws.

'This is a disaster!' she moaned. 'We couldn't find the baby and now we're stuck here with the deadly asteroid getting closer every second!'

At that moment, the air began to crackle with energy.

The squirrels stepped into the shadows.

Smoke swirled thickly through the trees.

PZAAP!

'It's coming back!' Ben exclaimed.

The time machine returned, jammed
with shapes inside.

'It's the Duke and Duchess,' Cassie said.
'Gertrude as well. And they've got the
baby dinosaur and the mummy one with
them.'

The glass lid opened with a hiss.

The Duke and Duchess sprang from the
time machine, followed a second later by
the time-travelling dinosaurs.

Gertrude was last out, splashing up to her
knees into a stagnant puddle and coating
her silk party frock with splats of mud.

'My dress!' she wailed. 'My shoes! This
is the worst day of my life!'

Gertrude turned to the dinosaurs, her
eyes narrowing.

'And, as for you two, get out of my sight!' the young girl snapped. 'You've already embarrassed me by being the most rubbish dinosaurs ever, so scram!'

'**MOOGLICK?**' the tiny dinosaur roared.

The farty blue smurf jumped on to its mother's back and the two of them cantered off into the jungle, happy to be where they belonged.

The Duke turned on the squirrels.

'Now, what's the meaning of this?' the Duke bellowed. 'We were waiting for our precious baby to be returned and out popped that dodgy actress!'

'What have you done with our son?' the Duchess hissed. 'He'd better be safe, that's all I can say.'

'Bubby nice,' Alfie said. 'Bubby goes googoogoogoo—'

'Will you kindly shut up?' the Duke said through clenched teeth. 'Now, where's our baby?'

Salty stepped forward.

'Babies are tougher than they look, pals,' Salty said. 'You're fretting for nothing! That babby'll turn up sooner or later.'

'Sooner or later?' the Duchess said. 'We want him back now, you flea-bitten rodent. He's one of the heirs to the Appleton millions.'

Salty pricked up his ears.

'Millions?' he said. 'The Appleton *millions*, eh? Are you saying old Salty will be getting a nice fat *reward* if he rescues your poor wee lost babby?'

The Duke leaned forward, his face scarlet with rage, his bulging nose touching Salty's snozzle.

'You want a *reward*?' he yelled. 'A *reward* for your utter *negligence* and squirrel-headed stupidity, letting my precious son loose in a world of drooling predators?'

'Aye, well, I'd settle for a sweet million,' Salty said, his eyes clouding as he dreamed of the cash.

'You'll settle for a sweet jab on the

nose if you don't find him!' the Duchess snarled.

At that very moment, the sound of leathery wings beat the air.

'The giant bats from the cave!' Ben cried.

The enormous creatures passed overhead, a squadron of furry flying beasts casting a shadow across the land.

'Alfie sees the baby!' Alfie shouted.

Alfie's sharp eyes were correct. The littlest of all Appletons was held by the biggest of the bats, kept aloft by a claw hooked into his nappy.

'Goooooooo!' the baby gurgled happily, eyes shining, waving down at the little crowd.

'My baby!' the Duchess gulped, waving fondly at the fast-vanishing baby. 'Stay brave, little angel!'

CHAPTER 21

BAT CRAZY

The bats flapped away, onwards and up towards the smoking cone of the brooding volcano which, rather unhelpfully, chose that precise moment to belch out a plume of deadly looking gas and smoke.

'What did I tell you, pals?' Salty said, smugly. 'Your wee one's perfectly safe.'

The Duke jabbed at Salty with his finger, flecks of spittle spraying from his mouth.

'Perfectly safe? PERFECTLY SAFE?! Our helpless sparkly-eyed babe held captive by a tribe of rabid bats, spirited off to an exploding volcano? And you say that's SAFE?'

'Ach! You'll laugh about this in years to come,' Salty said with a chuckle. 'Think what a story you'll have to tell!'

At that moment, a mud-covered dinosaur lumbered out of the forest.

Riding on its back was a human figure, clothes in tatters, hair awry.

'Fandango?' said the Duke.

'He's made friends with the Alamosaurus!' Ben said.

Fandango spat a mouthful of gunk on to the forest floor. The giant herbivore raised its long neck and got a pat of affection from the inventor.

'This helpful herbivore saved me,' Fandango said. 'We hid in a mud pool. Only way to escape the Velociraptors. Now, where's Rosalba?'

'She's sitting in my drawing room with a nice cup of tea, sixty-five million years in the future,' the Duchess said crisply.

'Typical!' Fandango scowled.

'Enough of this chitty-chat!' the Duke cried. 'We need to climb the volcano and save my son! Everyone together! Bring that dinosaur as well!'

Gertrude and Fandango muttered grumpily, but neither wanted to be left alone.

The expedition began to climb up through the tropical forest, breaking out on to the ashy slopes of the huge volcano. The Alamosaurus led the way, still missing its little baby friend.

Just then, a rumbling noise reached them. Deeper than thunder. Shaking the air.

'The volcano is waking up!' the Duchess said. 'Climb faster!'

A few volcanic bombs were ejected into the air, boulders crashing down into the forest at the base of the mountain.

'I hate this!' Gertrude moaned. 'It's typical of my baby brother to put us to all this trouble!'

The team increased their speed, puffing and panting as they trudged ever upwards, through the clinging ash.

The weary climbers (and stray Alamosaurus) made it to the lip of the volcano, where a most terrible sight awaited them.

A crater. A crater filled with bubbling,

molten lava. It blipped and blopped and flopped and flibbled, popping jets of melted rock high into the air.

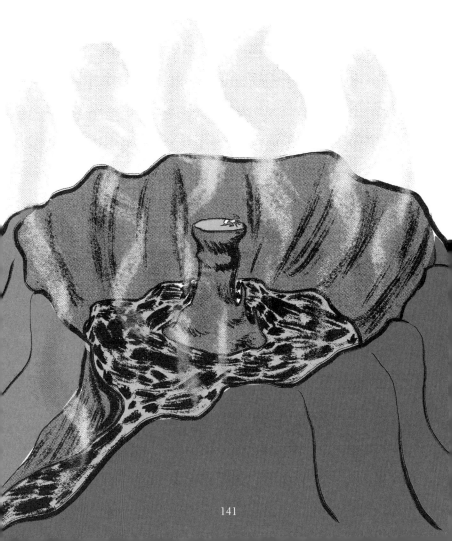

The sound of hissing gas echoed around the circular space.

Right in the middle of the lake was a tiny tower of rock, a finger of stone, jutting out in defiance of the hellish heat that surrounded it.

The top was a tiny area of safety just the size of a dinner table.

On that finger of rock was the baby.

The bats had flapped off.

He was utterly alone.

He was gurgling happily.

And he was crawling towards the edge.

'Do something!' the Duchess wailed. 'Quickly!'

Cassie and Ben put their heads together, thinking fast through the options.

'Only one way to rescue that little baby,' Cassie said. 'We use the Alamosaurus as a crane.'

'Perfect!' Ben agreed.

They whistled for the Alamosaurus, waiting impatiently as it slowly lumbered over to their position. The creature blurted an anguished grunt as it saw the peril the tiny baby was in.

Cassie jumped on to the creature's mighty neck. Ben followed, then Alfie. Salty whined about it, but he struggled on as well.

No commands were necessary. The dinosaur understood exactly what was needed.

Little by little, the Alamosaurus swung around, sticking that extraordinary neck far, far out over the bubbling lava. The heat was terrific, just like the blast from the open door of an oven.

'We'll have to be super-fast,' Cassie shouted above the blipping sound of the erupting bubbles, 'or we'll be frazzled alive!'

CHAPTER 22

CRATER RESCUE!

The Alamosaurus craned its neck to the limit and soon they were in position. The baby was right beneath them, crawling about the little finger of rock and cooing with delight as he spied the lava bubbles popping in all directions.

The Duke and Duchess watched from the crater rim, eyes wide, hearts aflutter. Even Gertrude was ashen-faced as she saw the peril her tiny brother was in.

'We're in the perfect spot,' Cassie cried. 'Form a squirrel chain!'

The squirrels shimmied forward until they were clinging just behind the creature's head. Ben grabbed a nostril, letting his legs flop down until he was dangling free.

Salty clambered down, holding on to Ben's foot for dear life, muttering and complaining non-stop. Cassie was next, and finally Alfie completed the chain.

'Go for it!' the Duke cried. 'There's not a second to lose!'

'To and fro!' Ben called. The squirrels began to swing.

The first pass missed. The second was almost there, but not quite – Alfie's paw swiping an arm's length from the baby's nappy.

'One more time!' Cassie instructed.

The squirrels swung back, clinging to each other for dear life as Alfie stretched to the limit.

'Alfie can't!' the tiny squirrel called.

The baby was still out of reach.

'I'll come and join the chain!' the Duchess called. 'It's the only chance!'

She lifted a leg to clamber on to the Alamosaurus, but the Duke reached out, holding her back.

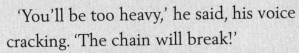

'You'll be too heavy,' he said, his voice cracking. 'The chain will break!'

For a few terrible moments, it seemed that all was lost.

Then the baby called out from his perilous tower.

'Get-ood!'

'He's speaking!' the Duke exclaimed with a sob. 'It's his first word!'

'Get-ood!' the baby cried again.

'It sounds like "get-ood",' the Duchess said with a frown. 'What a strange choice for his very first word.'

The baby called louder, his little face wreathed with a great smile as he waved at his sister.

'GET-OOD!'

Gertrude's eyes widened. The corners of her mouth twitched as she began to smile.

'He's saying my *name*,' she said with wonder. 'He's saying my *name*!'

Gertrude waved at her brother, her face suddenly alight with pleasure.

'Get-ood!' he cried.

'It's his first ever word, and it's ME! He's saying Gertrude!'

'Get-ood!' the baby sang.

The Duke and Duchess stared at their daughter, seeing a new light in her eyes.

'My little brother loves me after all!' Gertrude sighed.

The birthday girl stared fondly at her brother for a few more seconds, then raised her chin.

'I'm going to rescue him,' she said.

To the amazement of her parents, the young girl climbed on to the dinosaur's back.

'But, darling,' the Duchess said, 'it's incredibly risky. Are you sure?'

Gertrude nodded. 'He might be annoying,' she said, 'but he IS my brother.'

Moving at high speed, Gertrude scuttled along the dinosaur's neck and took just a scattering of seconds to reach the end. Hand over hand, she clambered down the chain of squirrels, the tiny creatures grunting as they strained to hold her weight.

'You'll have to be fast!' Cassie yelled.

Ben felt his grip begin to slip. 'Quickly!' he cried. 'Quick as you can!'

Salty's face went bright red with the strain, but he somehow held on.

Gertrude reached the bottom of the chain. She grabbed on to Alfie's foot,

lunging down towards her brother.

The baby stared up as he recognised his sister, hope shining in his eyes.

'Get-ood!' he called.

The dinosaur swung its neck. The crater lake blasted a great plume of molten lava. The rescuers gritted their teeth. The volcano roared with an earthly growl. Gertrude stretched down.

Success! Her fingers hooked into the baby's nappy!

'Thank goodness!' the Duchess gasped with relief as the Duke embraced her.

'I've got him!' Gertrude called.

'Baby safe! Baby happy!' Alfie called.

CHAPTER 23

ALAMOSAURUS DELIGHT

The mighty Alamosaurus turned away from the searing heat and back to the relative safety of the crater lip.

'My baby!' the Duchess cried.

Gertrude released her tiny brother and he snuggled into his mother's arms.

The squirrels fell in a heap into the soft ash, Gertrude collapsing next to them.

'You were so brave!' Cassie told the young girl.

'I'm proud of you all,' the Duke said. He swept them all into a hug, squirrels, Gertrude and dinosaur, until Salty broke free.

'Anything's possible, pals,' he crowed, 'when you've got the hero of the battle of Weasel Ridge on your team!'

The baby gurgled as it reached for the Alamosaurus, stretching a tiny hand to pet the awesome giant on the nose. The Alamosaurus made a happy grumbling noise, content to see its playmate safe once more.

The jubilant team of time travellers made their way back down the volcanic slopes. They pushed through the steamy jungle until they found the Pop-O-Matic.

Then Fandango frowned.

'There's a hole in the top,' he said. 'Must have been that eruption earlier. One of those volcanic rocks has smashed it.'

The friends inspected the machine.

'Can we still travel through time?' the Duke asked.

'I hope so.' Fandango scratched his head. 'But I'll have to fix that damage.'

The Duke stared upwards. The others followed his gaze.

Up in the sky, the asteroid was now brighter and closer, hotter even than the sun. A sinister trail of dark red cosmic dust trailed behind it. Across the steamy land, dinosaurs were gazing, eyes rolling, at the fast-moving ball of fire, grunting and bellowing at the unfamiliar sight.

'Impact in ten minutes, I reckon,' Ben said.

'We can't let the dinosaurs die!' Cassie muttered.

The Duchess raised her head and stared at Cassie.

'It's not just the dinosaurs that will be toast,' she said. 'We'll all be frazzled if Fandango can't sort this out.'

A terrific thumping noise came from the Pop-O-Matic.

Fandango called out.

'I need another hour to fix this. There'll be no time travel until it's done.'

'Well then,' the Duke said sadly, 'it looks like it might be the end for us all.'

The little group stared into the sky. The asteroid was now so luminous they

could hardly bear to look directly at it.
A strange, reddish, fiery light was cast
across the entire planet.

'It's going to zap us!' Ben said.

'We're all going to be sizzled!' Salty
yelled. 'We'll be vaporised, pals, vaporised
for sure!'

The Alamosaurus snorted, then
panicked at the sight of the approaching
asteroid. The sweet-natured dinosaur gave
the baby a lick on the nose and ran for the
jungle at high speed.

CHAPTER 24

SALTY SAVES THE DAY

'Seven minutes to impact, I reckon,' the Duke said gloomily.

'Think,' Ben said. 'There must be a solution.'

'I've got it!' Cassie exclaimed. 'We need to deflect the asteroid away from earth.

Why don't we create a giant Überpop and blast it into space?'

'Fantastic plan!' Ben enthused. 'If the Überpop is big enough and fast enough, it will knock that asteroid off course.'

Cassie snapped her fingers with delight. She turned to Fandango.

'Can the Pop-O-Matic still pop corn?' she asked.

'I guess so,' Fandango said doubtfully. 'But with that hole in the top, I'm not certain.'

'Where will you get unexploded corn?' the Duke asked.

Cassie pointed through the trees to the open field nearby where the wild corn was growing.

'We could use those freaky, giant-sized corn kernels!' she said.

'Brilliant strategy, pals!' Salty gasped. 'I was just about to say the same idea myself.'

'Überpop?' the Duchess snapped. 'What are you nutty squirrels yabbering about?'

'It's a sort of giant mutated popcorn,'
Fandango told the lady. 'It's horribly
huge and shoots out of the machine at
warp speed when the Pop-O-Matic gets
overloaded. It's a design flaw, to be honest,
but right now it could be just what we need.
It could nudge the asteroid off course!'

'It'll save us and the dinosaurs as well!'
Alfie yelled, dancing a little jig. 'It's the
best news ever!'

Cassie rushed through the jungle,
heading for the field.

'Come on, everyone! Grab as many
kernels as you can!' she called. The others
raced alongside her and soon they were
harvesting the super-sized corn, snapping
the heads from their stalks and rushing
back to dump their harvest into the Pop-
O-Matic.

Within two minutes they had placed
more than a hundred of the rugby-ball-
sized kernels into the popping zone of the
machine.

'Not enough!' Cassie cried. 'Keep loading.'

Fandango fired up the onboard generator of the Pop-O-Matic as the squirrels rushed back and forth into the field. A series of brilliant lights flashed across the side panel.

More wild corn went in.

The asteroid was now a flaming ball in the sky. Closer. Closer. Vibration and turbulence filled the air. The entire planet was beginning to shake.

The very air seemed to crackle with immense heat.

Herds of dinosaurs rushed in random directions; the forest was alive with the beating wings of giant bats.

On the Pop-O-Matic, cogs and engines buzzed. Fan belts fizzed into life.

'Ten more kernels!' Cassie yelled.

Ben and Alfie rushed up. The final giant corns were thrown in, the huge lid of the Pop-O-Matic slammed shut.

'It's going to be the biggest and most dangerous Überpop ever,' Fandango cried. 'Stand back!'

He slammed down a huge switch.

The machine juddered. The corn began to glow, devilish red, then neon green.

Out in space, the asteroid reached the final minute of its deadly journey. Countless squillions of tons of ice, rock and iron came tumbling out of the void, all set for a direct hit.

The Pop-O-Matic groaned. Steam raced from the place where the rocks had split the top.

The corn kernels trembled, but they did not pop.

'It's bad news!' Fandango called. 'It's losing pressure from that hole in the top. I'm not sure the Überpop can be created!'

'What can we do?' Cassie asked. 'Think quickly – there's not a second to lose!'

'We'll have to block it!' Fandango spluttered. 'It's the only answer. We need something large and extremely dense.'

'Leave it to me, pals,' Salty cried.

Salty jumped on to the mighty machine and wedged his backside into the hole.

'Get this, pals,' he yelled. 'Only a genuine 100-per-cent-Scottish backside can cure THIS problem!'

The pressure gauge wobbled, then flipped far into the red 'danger' zone.

'Er, Salty,' Cassie said.

'What?'

'You do know that you're about to be blasted into space?'

'Blasted into space?' Salty squeaked. 'What are you talking ab—'

An ear-splitting bang cut the air. The machine shuddered and groaned. The Überpop shot out of the Pop-O-Matic faster than a speeding bullet. As it accelerated, it expanded, almost as fast as the universe had done in the first milliseconds after the big bang. The hundreds of giant primeval popcorn kernels bonded together in a tungsten-hard crust, melting into an invincible force.

On top of the speeding Überpop was a tiny figure:

Salty!

Upright, eyes watering at the speed of the ascent, ears wobbling in the high velocity wind.

'Mammy!' he yelled.

'Go Salty!' Alfie yelled. 'You're my hero!'

CHAPTER 25

INFORMATION ALERT!

HOW SALTY BECAME (BRIEFLY) THE HEAVIEST, BEEFIEST, MOST DANGEROUS SQUIRREL IN THE UNIVERSE:

According to Einstein's laws, the faster something travels, the greater its mass becomes. This is due to the physics of Kinetic Energy, and as Salty approached 99.9999999 per cent of the speed of light, the equation looked like this:

Kinetic Energy (KE) is equal to half an object's mass (½ x m) multiplied by the Velocity (v) squared.

Light travels at 299,792,458 metres per second. Salty was travelling at 299,792,457 metres per second which means that:

Salty (2.4 kilograms) divided by two (1.2 kilograms) x 299,792,457 metres per second SQUARED equals an equivalent in joules to erm …

Erm …

Er …

More than 107 QUADRILLION joules.

That's the equivalent of more than 25 megatons (25 million tons of TNT).

$(1/2 \times m) \times v^2 = KE$

$(1/2 \times 2.4) \times 299{,}792{,}457^2$
$= 107{,}850{,}620{,}728{,}916{,}218.8$

Salty liked the feeling. In fact, it was the best feeling he'd ever had. As he zoomed out of the earth's atmosphere, his terror changed to raw aggression. His nerves evaporated as he saw the asteroid zooming towards him. Saltworthy McTavish Finnbar McNutt was about to pack the greatest punch in the history of the universe.

'I'll give you *asteroids*,' Salty growled.

He stood up on the Überpop as it rushed out of the earth's embrace. For a few brief moments, squirrel and tungsten-tipped popcorn were a single entity, locked together in a supersonic fiery cosmic embrace.

Salty scowled as he saw the flaming asteroid approach.

His eyes narrowed.

'Have some of this, pal!'

Salty clenched his knuckles.

'Think you're hard enough to mess with the hero of Weasel Ridge, do you?'

Salty's fist thudded into the asteroid.

A blinding white light swept the cosmos. Back on earth, the spectators shielded their eyes.

'Salty!' Alfie cried, his little lip trembling.

Down on the planet, a mighty roar cut through the air. The onlookers shook with the impact of it. Blazing light faded and died as the asteroid tumbled away from the earth, heading out into the vast void of space.

For a few seconds all was quiet.

'By Jove! He's done it!' the Duke whispered.

'Against all the odds,' Ben whispered. 'Salty saved the world.'

'The bravest squirrel ever,' Gertrude said.

'Rest in peace, Salty,' Cassie sobbed. 'We'll never forget you.'

'Alfie sad,' the littlest one murmured, a tear rolling down his little furry cheek. 'Alfie never see Salty again.'

'We should get out of here,' the Duchess said. 'How is the Pop-O-Matic looking now, Fandango?'

Fandango was inspecting the roof. 'We're in luck,' he exclaimed. 'The heat of the Überpop has melted the top back together. The hole has gone!'

The Duchess climbed into the time machine with her baby in her arms.

'Come along, Gertrude,' the Duke said. 'Come along, squirrels.'

Seconds later, the entire crew was on board.

Fandango reached out to the controls. Then he frowned.

'Hang on a minute,' he said. 'If Salty just

saved the dinosaurs from a terrible fate, he's probably changed the entire history of the planet. We could arrive back in our own time and find the earth still infested with dinosaurs!'

'There might not even be any humans!' the Duke said.

'Only one way to find out!' Gertrude said.

Fandango slammed down the lever and the journey began.

CHAPTER 26

SWEET ARRIVALS

The ballroom shimmered with a spooky light. Phantom wisps of dark green smoke filled the air.

SPLAT!

The Pop-O-Matic popped into existence in the middle of the floor.

The occupants emerged, footsteps crunching on the broken glass of the chandelier as they surveyed the ruins of Gertrude's party.

The Duke hugged his daughter. 'My sweet little bunny,' he said fondly. 'Your party was a bit of a nightmare, wasn't it? We'll make it up to you. You can have anything you like.'

'Anything I like?' Gertrude replied, her eyes glinting.

'Certainly!'

Gertrude smiled at her baby brother. He clutched at her hand and gurgled with pleasure.

'How about a family picnic, down by the lake?'

The Duke nodded, his eyes welling up with tears. The Duchess gave her daughter a big hug as the others clambered out of the time machine.

Fandango went to the window. 'This is odd. There don't seem to be any dinosaurs roaming around,' he observed.

The Duke was inspecting his fossil collection in the corner of the ballroom.

'By heavens!' the Duke cried. 'All these fossils have completely changed. All the rocks, all the amber, they've got odd little bits in them.'

The squirrels gathered round as the Duke examined his prize specimens.

'It's popcorn!' he exclaimed. 'These fossils are packed full of the stuff! But how on earth … ?'

'What goes up must come down,' the Duchess said. 'That Überpop deflected the asteroid, but perhaps that wasn't the end of the story.'

The Duke looked thoughtful. 'Yes. The Überpop must have travelled through space for a while and then crashed back down to earth and wiped out the dinosaurs after all. A kind of popcorn Armageddon.'

Cassie was inspecting the fossils. 'Wait!' she cried. 'What's this?'

She picked up a smooth piece of amber. The other squirrels clustered in close to stare at the translucent yellow stone.

Captured inside it was an insect.

'It's a flea!' Cassie said.

'A flea?' the Duke snorted. 'There were no fleas like that one in the time of the dinosaurs!'

'It must be one of Salty's fleas!' Ben said.

The squirrels stared in wonder at the tiny insect, locked in the grip of the fossilised resin.

'If it's bitten Salty, it'll have Salty's DNA inside it,' the Duke said.

'The DNA could be extracted,' the Duchess added. 'Like they did in the *Jurassic Park* movie. Salty could be cloned from the DNA. He could be recreated!'

'Salty could live again!' Cassie exclaimed.

At that moment, Rosalba strutted into the ballroom.

'Are you sure about that?' she said with a loud sniff. 'Isn't the world better off without him?'

'It will be a fascinating experiment,' the Duke pronounced. 'I'll happily pay for the cloning to take place.'

The Duke drove the squirrels to a science park not far from town. There, behind the gleaming glass panels of a hi-tech building, a company by the name of Clones R Us agreed to take on the delicate task of cloning Salty.

'There might be side effects,' the boss told them. 'But we'll give it a go.'

'Side effects?' Cassie asked. 'What type of side effects?'

The boss bit his lip. 'There's no way of telling. But we'll know within twenty-four hours,' he concluded. 'Come back tomorrow and we'll see if your friend Salty can be cloned back to life!'

CHAPTER 27

JUMPING JACK SALTY

The squirrels gathered the following afternoon for the unveiling.

The head of the science institute opened the door to the vast cloning machine.

A light flashed.

Pipes gushed with a hiss of compressed air.

A creature emerged. A creature that looked, and smelled, exactly like Salty.

'Yay! Salty's been cloned off a flea!' Alfie yelled. 'Alfie happy again!'

Salty stood blinking at the spectators, slightly shaky on his feet.

'Cloned off a flea?' he snarled. 'What rubbish are you talking? If Salty was going to be cloned, he'd be cloned off a great white shark, pals, or a ferocious pit bull!'

Salty scratched his fur. Then he hopped.
Then he hopped again.

'Oh dear,' the scientist said.

'You're hopping!' Ben said with a
snigger. 'Hopping like a flea!'

Salty hopped even higher.

'I'm not, pals,' he protested. 'It's just a
new way of walking that I've invented.'

'Salty half flea!' Alfie cried. Tears of laughter rolled down his little fluffy cheeks.

Salty stopped hopping: 'Actually,' he said, 'I do feel different in one way. I'm a new *improved* Salty now. Even more heroic! No more temper tantrums.'

Cassie and Ben shared a knowing look.

'So … if someone stole your popcorn, you'd just give them a nice smile, would you?' Cassie said.

'Aye,' Salty confirmed, 'probably help them to pack it up in a wee paper bag.'

'And if someone said you were a scabby, flea-infested squirrel scallywag with porridge for brains?' Ben suggested.

Salty laughed lightly. 'Ha ha! I'd just wink at that jolly prankster and give him a merry laugh before skipping happily on my way. It would wash over me, pals; I'm above that now!'

'What about a *weasel*?' Alfie cried.

Salty's eye twitched.

'A *what*?' he snapped.

'A weeeeasel,' Alfie continued. 'A great big massive, *furry* weeeeeasel.'

'Yes,' Ben continued, 'what about a weasel that said all your stories about the battle of Weasel Ridge were *lies*?'

Salty's teeth began to grind together with a horrible crunching noise.

His paws clenched tight.

'What about a weasel that said that HE was the true hero of the battle of Weasel Ridge and it wasn't you at all?' Cassie suggested.

Salty's ear wobbled.

His eyes rolled.

'Where is he?' he roared.

Salty slammed his sweaty foot on the ground.

'Show me him! Where is he? I'll put his tail in a soup! I'll teach him a lesson he'll never forget! I'll run him out of town with his weasel clan! I'll load my special machine gun with acorns just like I did

that day on Weasel Ridge and I'll rat-a-tat-tat-tat-tat until there's not a weasel left in … '

Salty hopped up and down, ranting and raving about weasels and why he hated them until his voice started to get hoarse.

'I don't like to interrupt,' Cassie said, 'but I think we've proved we've got the same old Salty back. And besides, I'm hungry!'

'Me too!' Ben said. 'All those adventures in the time of the dinosaurs have left me in the mood for just one thing … '

Alfie smiled.

Cassie smiled.

Salty … almost … smiled.

Ben gave them a big hug.

Then they all licked their lips.

'POPCORN!' they yelled.

The next great adventure was about to begin!

THE END